Starring in

Just a Little Extra

D0094132

Starring in
Just a Little Extra

By **Ellen Conford**
Illustrated by **Renee W. Andriani**

Simon & Schuster Books for Young Readers
New York   London   Toronto   Sydney   Singapore

SIMON & SCHUSTER BOOKS FOR YOUNG READERS
An imprint of Simon & Schuster Children's Publishing Division
1230 Avenue of the Americas, New York, New York 10020

Book design by Anahid Hamparian
The text of this book is set in 15 point Berkeley Book.
Printed in the United States of America
10 9 8 7 6 5 4 3 2 1

Library of Congress Cataloging-in-Publication Data
Conford, Ellen.
Annabel the actress starring in just a little extra / by Ellen Conford; illustrations by
Renée W. Andriani.—1st ed.
p.   cm.
Summary: When she learns that a famous director is making a movie in her home
town, ten-year-old Annabel is determined to get a part in it.
ISBN 0-689-81405-4
[1. Actors and actresses—Fiction. 2. Motion pictures—Production and direction—
Fiction.] I. Williams-Andriani, Renée, ill. II. Title.
PZ7.C7593Ap   2000   [Fic]—dc21   99-23490

The black-and-white illustrations for this book were done with crowquill
pen and ink. The jacket art is pen-and-ink colored with watercolor and
artists' dyes.

Scene One:

Friday Afternoon, Hudson Street

Annabel was an actress. She wasn't famous yet. She wasn't a star. But she knew someday she would be.

Meanwhile, she practiced her acting all the time.

Today on the way home from school, she stopped in the middle of the street. She turned to her best friend, Maggie. She put her hand over her eyes.

"I'm all alone," she moaned. "All, all alone."

"No, you're not," Maggie said. "I'm here."

"I am a pitiful orphan," Annabel insisted. She squeezed her eyes shut. She made a little sobbing sound.

"I have no mother and father. I haven't a friend in the world."

"You're acting, aren't you?" Maggie asked.

Annabel took her hand from her eyes.

"I was practicing Loneliness. Did you feel sorry for me?"

"Um—not very," Maggie had to admit.

"You're right," Annabel said. "I didn't really *feel* the loneliness."

"Maybe you need to suffer more," Maggie suggested.

"I think I'd rather just practice more," Annabel said.

They stopped at the corner of Hudson Street to wait for the walk signal.

Just as the light changed, a truck zoomed past them. It was white, with a tree painted on the side. The tree had round leaves, like silver dollars.

"Hey! Where's the fire?!" Maggie yelled as the truck sped off.

"I've seen that truck somewhere." Annabel stared after it as it screeched around the corner onto Central Avenue.

She closed her eyes, and tried to remember.

"Silver tree . . . Silver—" Her eyes snapped open.

"In the movies!" she said. "Silver Tree is a movie company!"

"What's a movie company doing here?" Maggie asked.

"Making a movie!"

Annabel shrieked so loud that the beagles who lived in the corner house started to howl.

"Why would anyone want to make a movie in Westfield?" Maggie wondered.

"They make movies in lots of places," Annabel said. She was so excited she couldn't stand still. "Not just in Hollywood."

She grabbed Maggie by the shoulders. "And sometimes they use regular, ordinary people!"

"Wow!" Maggie suddenly understood what Annabel was thinking. "You mean—"

"Yes!" Annabel shouted. "This could be it! My Big Break!"

She let go of Maggie's shoulders. She raced off down Hudson Street.

"Where are you going?" Maggie yelled.

She caught up with Annabel on Central Avenue.

They heard a loud engine behind them. A huge eighteen-wheeler rumbled past. A flatbed truck trailed after it. Both trucks had silver trees on their doors.

"I knew it!" Annabel cried. "Follow those trucks!"

The two trucks continued down Central Avenue. They stopped across from the Westfield Shopping Plaza, right near the entrance to Memorial Park.

When Annabel saw what was happening on Central Avenue, she froze. She clutched Maggie's hand.

"Pinch me," she said. "I think I must be dreaming."

Scene Two:

Friday Afternoon, Westfield Plaza

A row of Silver Tree trucks were parked around the Plaza. Workers were unloading cameras and lights and microphones.

A crowd was already forming near the park. A police officer was directing the traffic that inched down Central Avenue.

Annabel saw a light blue van with a News 10 symbol near the park entrance. A woman with a microphone stood next to the van, talking to a short, chubby man in a baseball cap.

Behind them, a bunch of kids were clowning around. They waved and made rabbit ears with their fingers. A woman with a minicam tried to shoo them away.

"Oh, good," Annabel said. "The media is here. Now we will find out what's going on."

She pulled Maggie toward the news van.

"This is Lisa Diaz," the woman with the microphone was saying. "With me is Buzz Barlow. Buzz is the second assistant director of *The Day After Doom*."

"Sounds scary," Maggie said.

"Buzz," Lisa Diaz began, "isn't this the first TV movie Steven Roth has ever made?"

Annabel gasped. Steven Roth! He was the most famous director in America!

"I think so," Buzz Barlow said.

"And are you going to shoot some scenes for the movie right here in Westfield?"

"Yeah," said Buzz Barlow.

Annabel punched her fist in the air. "YES!"

"Hold it!" Lisa Diaz turned and glared at her. "I am not interviewing *you*," she said sharply.

"Sorry." Annabel put her hand over her mouth and tiptoed backward.

"Mr. Barlow," Lisa began again, "will you be using any of our Westfield citizens in the movie?"

"We'll want some extras," Buzz said. "For the crowd scenes."

Annabel screamed. She hugged Maggie so hard that Maggie squealed.

Lisa Diaz stamped her foot. "Get back!" she snarled at Annabel. She raised her microphone like a hatchet. "Get away from me!"

"Sorry," Annabel said meekly. "It won't happen again."

The camerawoman changed her position. She tried to keep the group of rowdy kids behind her.

Lisa Diaz started her questions over.

Annabel edged toward Buzz Barlow. She didn't want to miss a word.

"When will James Lockwood and Winona McCall be here?" Lisa asked.

"Winona McCall!" Annabel fell onto Maggie's shoulder. *"Winona McCall!"* she screamed.

Lisa Diaz hurled her microphone halfway across Central Avenue. *"Get that kid out of here!"*

Annabel barely heard her.

Winona McCall was *the* hot young actress. She had already won an Oscar for *Swimming to Paradise*. She was beautiful and dark and fiery. Her acting was so realistic, you forgot she was acting.

She was Annabel's hero.

"Pinch me again," Annabel whispered to Maggie. "I can't believe I'm going to be in a movie with Winona McCall."

"But you haven't even got a part yet," Maggie said.

"I will get a part," Annabel said.

"I can't work this way!" Lisa Diaz turned her back on everyone, and climbed into the News 10 van.

Buzz Barlow shrugged. He started toward the Silver Tree trucks.

Annabel hurried after him. "Mr. Barlow?"

He didn't seem to hear her.

An actor has to *project*, Annabel reminded herself.

Projecting meant speaking loud enough to be heard in the last row of a theater.

"MR. BARLOW!" she projected. She dashed in front of him. She planted herself right in his path. He couldn't miss her.

"MR. BARLOW! I HAVE TO TALK TO YOU!"

He looked down. He frowned. His baseball cap and T-shirt had *The Day After Doom* printed on them.

Maybe I'll get a T-shirt, Annabel thought, *when I start work in the movie.*

18

"What is it?" Buzz Barlow sounded annoyed.

No wonder he's annoyed, Annabel thought. *All those pesky kids hassling him.*

"I am an actress," she announced.

He snorted. "Who isn't?"

He tried to move around her.

She jumped sideways and blocked his path.

"And I need my Big Break," she said.

"Listen, kid, I don't have time to—"

"*Please,* Mr. Barlow." Annabel looked up at him desperately. "You're the first second assistant director I've ever met."

"Huh?"

She read the words on his shirt. "*The Day After Doom,*" she said. "That sounds like the movie will be scary. I do great Fear."

"Huh?"

"And I am an excellent screamer," she went on. "Would you like to hear my scream?"

"No," Buzz said.

"But, Mr. Barlow—"

"Come back tomorrow."

"You mean it?" Annabel could have hugged him. "You're going to give me a part?"

"Just come back tomorrow," he said.

"Oh, thank you!" Annabel cried. "What time tomorrow?"

"I don't know," he said. "Early. Now will you please leave me alone?"

Annabel raced back to Maggie.

"I got a part!" she shouted.

Maggie's mouth dropped open. "I don't believe it. You got discovered?"

"Well," Annabel said, "maybe not exactly discovered. But maybe very close to being *almost* discovered."

Scene Three:

Friday Night, Annabel's Living Room

"You got a role in a movie just like that?" Annabel's father said. He'd been saying it all evening.

"It wasn't just like that," Annabel kept telling him. "I've waited a long time for my Big Break."

"I know, but—" Her father shook his head, puzzled. "Weren't there any tryouts? Didn't you have to sign anything?"

"So far, I think I'm just an extra," Annabel said. "Maybe you don't have to sign anything till you get a speaking part."

They had watched the Channel 10 News at Six. Lisa Diaz had gotten an interview with Steven Roth himself.

He'd said that *The Day After Doom* was about a deadly poison cloud. He'd said that Winona McCall would arrive in Westfield tomorrow.

At that, Annabel had screamed. She slid off the couch in a pretend faint.

"We *must* go to the video store," she said. "I have to watch some scary movies so I can practice."

"Practice what?" her father asked.

"Being part of a terrified mob," she said. "Did you know that that's how Winona McCall was discovered?"

"She was discovered in a mob scene?" her father asked.

"Not exactly," Annabel said. "She got killed in *In Sickness and in Death*." Annabel knew everything about Winona McCall. "All she did was scream and die. And she got discovered."

"That's amazing," Annabel's father said.

"That's show business," Annabel said.

Later Annabel looked at the three Timeless Terror Treats she had rented.

"I'll watch *Nandor the Gila Monster* first." She pushed the cassette into the VCR. "He's the mother of all monsters."

She'd never heard of Nandor. But that's what it said on the video box.

Annabel's mother came into the living room.

"What are you watching?" she asked.

"A Timeless Terror Treat," Annabel said.

A preview for *Attack of the Slime People* began.

"I think I'll go clean the attic," her mother said.

Annabel settled back on the couch. Her father sat down next to her.

The titles for *Nandor the Gila Monster* started rolling.

"Agghh!" Annabel screamed.

Her father jumped sideways. "What are you screaming at?" he asked. "The titles aren't scary."

"I was just warming up," Annabel said.

Her father sighed.

Nandor turned out to be a Japanese movie with English subtitles.

"How can I read the movie and practice

Fear at the same time?" Annabel said, annoyed.

"Quietly, I hope," her father answered.

Annabel didn't think Nandor was especially scary. But that was okay. Tomorrow she'd have to act scared, even when she really wasn't.

So she practiced scaring herself.

She pictured a huge, horrible-smelling green cloud. It was coming toward her. It was growing bigger and bigger.

She smelled the hideous smell. She felt the sickening vapor press against her face.

She clutched at her throat. "ACK-ACK-ARRGGHH!" She coughed harshly. She turned her face into a gruesome mask of terror.

"I can't hear the movie," her father complained, "with you shrieking like that."

"There's nothing to hear," Annabel said. "It's in Japanese."

Finally, after twenty minutes of Annabel's screaming, choking, and fainting, her father got off the couch.

"Where are you going?" Annabel asked.

"Upstairs," her father said. "I think I'll see what they're selling on the Shop Till You Drop Network."

"But you'll miss the scary parts," Annabel said.

"You've scared me enough already," her father said.

Annabel beamed. "Thank you!"

It took ages till terrified crowds started to stampede through the city. When Nandor finally invaded downtown Tokyo, Annabel was more than ready.

She made her eyes huge. She pushed her

hands out in front of her. She screamed her
most blood-curdling scream.

She staggered backward. She fell over a
footstool and landed on her head.

"OW!"

"Annabel, *please,*" her mother called from
upstairs. "Your acting is giving me a
headache."

"Me too," said Annabel.

By ten o'clock, Annabel decided she'd
done enough practicing.

She had studied terrified faces in nine
crowd scenes. She had a bump on the back
of her head. Her throat was sore from
screaming.

She needed to rest her voice. She didn't want to be screamed out when it came time to shoot her scene.

She went upstairs to say good-night to her parents. They were in bed, with the TV on.

"What are you watching?" Annabel perched on the edge of the bed.

"*American Almanac,*" her mother said. "They're at the Soapstone, Minnesota Cheese Carving Festival."

Annabel peered at the screen. She saw something big and yellow. It looked like a fire hydrant with arms. And a guitar.

"What's that supposed to be?" she asked.

"Elvis Presley," her father answered. "Sculpted entirely out of cheddar cheese."

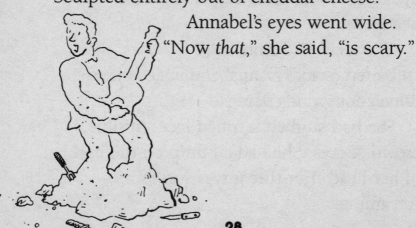

Annabel's eyes went wide. "Now *that*," she said, "is scary."

Scene Four:

Saturday Morning, Annabel's House and Westfield Plaza

Maggie rang the doorbell at 7:30 the next morning. Her older brother, Oliver, was with her.

Maggie wanted to see Annabel act in her first movie. Oliver wanted to see Winona McCall.

Maggie looked Annabel up and down. "Why are you wearing that?" she asked.

Maggie was a very stylish dresser. She planned to be a fashion designer. She was always sketching ideas for outfits.

Today she wore a long flowered skirt and a pink T-shirt. She had a floppy-brimmed hat with a big pink rose on it.

Annabel was dressed in red shorts and an old white top with ruffled straps.

She had red flip-flops on her feet. The flip-flops were half a size too big.

"I think your shirt shrank," Oliver said.

"I dressed young," Annabel explained. "So I'd look more pitiful."

"You look pretty pitiful," Oliver said.

"Great!" Annabel said. "Thank you."

As they walked down Hudson Street, Annabel explained what she had learned from watching terrified crowd scenes all last evening.

"When the monster comes," Annabel said, "no one cares if he kills a teenager."

"Hey!" Oliver protested. Oliver was thirteen.

"But a little kid looks helpless and pathetic," Annabel went on. "A kid in danger is *always* heartbreaking."

Halfway to Westfield Plaza the road was blocked by wooden barricades.

A police officer was directing the backed-up traffic to side streets.

Cars were crawling into the Plaza parking lot. The sidewalks were jammed with people. They spilled into the street, bumped into one

another, and dodged in between cars.

Horns blared. Drivers yelled at each other, at the crowds clogging the road, and at the police officer.

"I never knew so many people wanted to be actors," Maggie said.

"They don't want to be actors," Annabel said scornfully. "They just want to be movie stars."

They followed the crowd around Locust Drive.

"I can't believe I'm going to meet Winona McCall." Just saying Winona's name made Annabel's heart skip.

"Yeah," Oliver agreed. "She's a babe."

"She's *not* a babe!" Annabel was outraged. "She's an actor."

"Okay, okay," said Oliver. "So she's an actor babe."

There were so many people around them that Annabel couldn't see Central Avenue until she reached the very end of Locust Drive.

When she finally saw the activity in front of Westfield Plaza, all she could do was stare.

She had stepped into another world.

Tall banks of lights were set up on both sides of the street. A big crane with a seat swinging from it towered over the Plaza. There were microphones on poles and cameras on wheels.

Near the entrance to Memorial Park, a large crowd gathered behind wooden barriers.

Oliver looked around eagerly for Winona McCall.

"Look!" He pointed. "There's her chair."

A row of director's chairs were lined up on the sidewalk. WINONA MCCALL was stenciled on one of them.

Annabel gazed at Winona's name.

"I wish I could sit in it," she said. "Just for a minute."

"Someday you'll have your own chair," Maggie said. "With your own name on it."

Annabel thought about that for a moment.

"I think it should be eggshell white," Maggie said. "With black letters."

"Yes," Annabel said softly. "I can see it."

A woman wearing a *Day After Doom* T-shirt stepped in front of them.

"You can't be here," the woman said. "We're shooting."

The woman had a plastic picture ID on a black cord around her neck. The name under the picture was JEAN FURMAN.

"I'm supposed to be here," Annabel said. "I am an actress."

"That's nice," the woman said. "But you can't stay on the set. You'll have to wait over there." She pointed to the crowd in front of the park.

"But Buzz Barlow *personally* told me to come," Annabel said.

"That's right." Maggie nodded.

"Did he?" Jean Furman flipped through a bunch of papers on her clipboard. "What's your name?"

"Annabel," Annabel said.

"There's no Annabel on my list," the woman said.

"But I met him yesterday," Annabel insisted. "And he told me to come back today."

Jean Furman laughed. She shook her head and stuck her clipboard under her arm.

"Now I get it," she said. "Honey, he told *everyone* to come back today."

Scene Five:

Saturday Morning, Westfield Plaza

"What?" Annabel's heart sank.

"We might use you as an extra," Jean Furman said. "But you still have to wait with the others."

Annabel was crushed. "I thought I already *was* an extra."

"She's really a great actor," Maggie said. "And she practiced Fear all night."

"Sorry," the woman said. "Behind the barriers, please."

"Rats," Oliver said. He slouched off toward the park.

"Go on, girls!" Jean Furman put her hand on Annabel's shoulder and gave her a little push.

This is how an orphan really feels, Annabel thought. *This is what it's like when nobody wants you.*

She had to do something. This was supposed to be her Big Break. She might only get one Big Break in her whole life.

But what could she do?

All she felt like doing was crying.

No, she told herself. *I will not cry.*

What good would crying do? They didn't need sad people for this movie. They needed scared people.

Scared people.

Suddenly Annabel knew what she had to do.

She screamed. Very loudly.

"No! No, get away!" She whirled out of Jean Furman's grasp and ran.

"Help me! Help me!" She raced across Central Avenue.

Everyone on the set stopped working.

Annabel could feel hundreds of eyes on her.

She staggered toward Winona McCall's chair.

She clawed at her throat. With a terrible groan, she slumped to the ground.

She heard shouting and running feet.

She felt people huddling around her.

"Annabel!" Maggie's voice. "What's wrong with you?"

Annabel kept her eyes closed. She tried to look pale.

"What happened to this little girl?"

That voice! Annabel knew that voice. The rich, musical tones. The perfect pronunciation.

Gentle fingers touched Annabel's wrist.

"I think she's unconscious."

Annabel let her eyelids flutter a little.

"Ohhh," she moaned softly.

Slowly, very slowly, she opened her eyes.

Scene Six:

Saturday Morning, On the Set of THE DAY AFTER DOOM

A circle of worried faces peered down at her.

Winona McCall was kneeling at her shoulder.

"You're safe," Winona said. "You must have fainted."

Annabel gazed up at her hero. She was so dazzled she wasn't sure she could speak.

"Oh, Miss McCall," she whispered. "I've always wanted to meet you."

She sat up and opened her eyes all the way.

"Do you feel dizzy?" Winona McCall asked.

Steven Roth himself stood over her.

Annabel jumped to her feet. She brushed off her shorts.

"I feel fine," she said cheerfully. "I didn't really faint."

"Annabel!" Maggie said. "You scared me."

"Did I really?" Annabel asked. "Oh, good."

Steven Roth glared at her. "Just what do you think you're doing, young lady?"

"Acting," said Annabel.

"Acting?" He scowled. "I haven't got time for games."

"Mr. Roth," Annabel began seriously, "my acting is not a game. I had to get you to notice me.

"I noticed you," he growled. "*Everybody* noticed you."

"Well, finally." Annabel sighed. "I've been waiting to be discovered for years."

Winona McCall threw back her head and laughed. It was the most beautiful laugh Annabel had ever heard.

"How long could you have been waiting?" the director asked. "You're only—what? Eight years old?"

"Ten," Annabel said. "I dressed young."

"All right, kid." Buzz Barlow was glaring down at her. "You've held us up long enough."

"Steven," Winona said softly. "She's a very promising actor."

Annabel thought she might really faint. She was a promising actor! Winona McCall herself had said so!

"She's a pain in the neck," Steven Roth said.

"But you believed her," Winona said. "So did I."

"She was screaming like a crazy person," Mr. Roth grumbled.

"Then why not let her scream something?" Winona suggested.

Annabel thought her heart would stop. "A *speaking* part?" she gasped. "You want to give me a speaking part?"

"Well," Winona said and grinned, "maybe a screaming part."

"Okay, okay!" Steven Roth gave in. "She can scream something. Whatever it takes to get this show on the road."

Annabel screamed.

"Not now!" the director exploded.

Scene Seven:

Saturday Afternoon, On the Set of THE DAY AFTER DOOM

Two hours later Annabel was beginning to think her part of the show would *never* get on the road.

She was waiting with the crowd near the park. But it wasn't much of a crowd anymore.

The sun was blazing. A lot of people had gotten hot and bored, and gone home.

Oliver kept complaining that he'd missed meeting Winona McCall. He kept complaining about how bored he was.

Annabel was finding it hard to wait for her screaming part. But she wasn't bored.

She'd watched as Winona McCall was

dabbed with water to make her look sweaty. She'd watched as James Lockwood patrolled Central Avenue, holding a gray metal box.

"The scanner must be broken," he said. "I've never seen a reading like this."

He said it four times.

"Do all movies take so long to make?" Maggie asked.

"Steven Roth is a *very* demanding director," Annabel answered.

At last, Buzz Barlow came over to the group that was left behind the barricades.

"Attention, everyone! It's showtime!"

He explained what the extras were supposed to do in the crowd scene.

"The poison cloud will be up there." He pointed to the sky. "Everyone listen for Annabel to scream. Then, look up at the cloud, and run toward the park."

Annabel felt a shiver of pride. She was the key person in the whole scene! The action couldn't start without her scream!

"The cloud is going to be up there?" Oliver looked toward Locust Drive. "I don't see anything."

"You won't see it," Buzz said. "We'll do the cloud in special effects."

"Rats!" said Oliver. "What a cheat."

"Now, Annabel," Buzz Barlow helped her duck under the wooden barrier. "Come with me."

Annabel's heart raced in her chest. This was it! Her first movie!

Her flip-flops went *thwuck-thwuck* as Buzz led her into the middle of Central Avenue.

She hoped the sounds wouldn't mess up the scene.

Jean Furman and another man started placing the other extras around the shopping area. They directed them into doorways, and in front of store windows.

Steven Roth was up in the crane seat.

"Okay, people!" he yelled through a bullhorn. "It's just a normal Saturday at the mall. You're talking, you're shopping. Everything is perfectly ordinary."

Annabel was so nervous she thought she might not even have to act scared.

"Annabel," Steven Roth called. "You'll be crossing the street. When you get your cue, you scream and start running."

"Okay!"

"The rest of you people, wait for Annabel to scream," the director said. "Then you panic and run to the park."

I'm panicking already, Annabel thought.

She had not needed to spend all that time last night practicing Fear.

She had never been so nervous in her life.

"Let's do it!" Steven Roth yelled.

"Rolling!" someone shouted.

"Scene 83! Take one!"

"ACTION!"

"Go, Annabel!"

Scene Eight:

Saturday Afternoon, On the Set of THE DAY AFTER DOOM

Annabel looked up into the sky. She screamed.

"CUT!"

Oh, no, she thought. *What did I do wrong?* She looked up at Steven Roth in the crane seat.

"Annabel!" he called. "Don't scream right away. First, stare at the cloud. Wonder what it could be. Then get scared."

Whew! Annabel thought. He didn't sound mad. He just sounded like a director.

"Scene 83! Take two!"

"ACTION!"

Annabel looked up at the sky.

She opened her eyes wide. *I see the*

poison cloud, she imagined. *It's huge! It's terrifying!*

I'm doomed!

She screamed.

"CUT!"

"Oh, no!" Annabel cried. "Did I do it wrong again?"

"People!" Steven Roth yelled. "You're not statues! Move around. It's a busy Saturday at the mall. Look busy! Walk. Talk. Window shop!"

Annabel breathed a deep sigh of relief. The director wasn't yelling at her.

"Good job, Annabel!" he yelled suddenly.

She jumped.

"Do it that way again."

Annabel glowed with Mr. Roth's praise. *She was good.*

They did it again. And again.

She was finding it hard to feel fear so many times in a row. And she was a little worried about her flip-flops. They kept making those funny *thwuck-thwuck* sounds every time she ran across the street.

Maybe she should have worn sneakers.

But no one complained about the flip-flops, and no one but Annabel seemed to notice they were making noise.

Buzz Barlow and Jean kept moving people around.

Steven Roth kept yelling, "One more time!"

"One more time!" he yelled, for the eighth time.

Annabel tested her voice. "Hmm, hmm, hmm." She hoped she could still get a piercing scream out.

"*Day After Doom!* Scene eighty-three! Take eight!"

"ACTION!"

"*Go, Annabel!*"

Annabel looked up. She pictured the cloud. She stared. She opened her mouth. She screamed as loud as she could.

No one yelled "CUT!"

She started to run.

She ran across Central Avenue.

Her flip-flops felt like there was glue on their bottoms. They were sticking to the hot street.

Annabel's foot twisted under her. She tried to keep from falling, but she couldn't get her balance.

She sprawled onto the sidewalk.

"Oh, no!" she cried.

The terrified crowd stampeded past her.

"No! *No!*"

She tried to get up. Someone kicked her in her twisted ankle.

She rolled onto her side, and burst into tears.

"CUT! PRINT IT!"

Scene Nine:

Saturday Afternoon,
Central Avenue

"*What?*" Annabel couldn't believe she had heard right.

"Good work, people," Steven Roth said. "Thanks a lot. Hope you like the movie."

The crane seat swooped down, and the director jumped out.

Annabel limped over to him.

"My shoe fell off," she said. "Aren't you going to do the scene over?"

He shook his head. "I got what I wanted."

He spotted her red flip-flop near the curb. He picked it up and brought it to her.

"But I fell down," Annabel insisted. "I ruined the shot."

"You were fine." He patted her on the shoulder and walked away.

"Pack it up, everyone!" he called.

Annabel heard Winona McCall's voice behind her. "So how did it feel to be in your first movie?"

She turned around, and looked up at her idol.

"Awful," she said. "I messed up."

The crew was already loading equipment onto the trucks.

Maggie and Oliver ran over to Annabel.

"Are you okay?" Maggie asked anxiously.

Oliver didn't even look at Annabel. He just stood there, staring at Winona McCall.

"Not very," Annabel said. "They'll cut me

out of the scene. Just when I thought I was going to get discovered."

Winona McCall touched Annabel's cheek. "I'm sure you'll be discovered one of these days," she said.

Annabel felt her heart thump. She was so thrilled she almost forgot her disappointment.

"Do you really think so?" she asked.

Winona smiled. Maggie stared. Oliver had not stopped staring.

"Of course," Winona said.

"Oh, Ms. McCall." Annabel could hardly get the words out. "Meeting you was even more exciting than being in a movie."

Oliver finally found his voice. "Especially since you loused up your part," he said.

Maggie jabbed him with her elbow. "Was anyone talking to *you*?"

"Just keep trying, Annabel," Winona said. "You'll make it. And I hope you remember me when you win your first Oscar."

For the second time that day Annabel thought she might faint.

Scene Ten:

Four Months Later, Annabel's Living Room

"You're sure the VCR is working?" Annabel asked.

"I'm sure," her father said.

Annabel was frantic. *The Day After Doom* would be on in five minutes.

She wasn't sure she could wait that long.

Maggie and Oliver had come to watch the movie with Annabel and her parents.

"I hope they'll show a little of my scream," Annabel said. "Before I fell down."

The movie finally started. Annabel could hardly follow the story. Of course, she watched closely every time Winona McCall was on the screen.

But she was so worried about her own

part, it was hard to concentrate. Would she
be in the movie at all? Would anyone ever
hear her scream?

Winona played a scientist. For the first
fifteen minutes of the movie she wore a white
lab coat.

"She's a babe," Oliver said. "Even in that
dorky scientist outfit."

"She's not a babe!" Annabel snapped.

"I wish this was on tape already," Maggie
said. "Then we could fast forward to your
part."

"If I have a part," Annabel said glumly.

Winona studied a map. She looked
worried.

Two sets of commercials interrupted the movie.

They had been watching for forty-five minutes when—suddenly—a shot of Central Avenue filled the screen.

There was Westfield Plaza! There was Memorial Park!

Annabel screamed. Maggie screamed. Oliver said, "Hey."

The camera pulled back and up. A dirty gray-green mushroom-shaped cloud moved across the sky.

"So that's the cloud," Oliver said. "It's not very scary."

The camera focused on Central Avenue again. The extras walked back and forth in front of the stores.

Annabel held her breath. She squeezed her hands together.

They cut me out, she worried to herself. *I'm sure they cut me out.*

Suddenly she saw her face. Right in the middle of the TV screen.

"It's me!" she yelled. "It's *me!*"

Maggie cheered. Annabel's parents cheered. Oliver said, "Hey."

Annabel couldn't breathe. She leaned forward and watched the Annabel in the movie.

She saw her eyes grow wide. She saw a look of terror spread over her face. She heard herself scream.

And then she was gone.

The camera cut to the terrified mob. It followed as they charged across the street and into the park.

"You were so good," her mother said.

"But I was only on for two seconds." Annabel slumped down on the couch. "Two seconds isn't long enough to get discovered."

Oliver was still watching the movie.

"Here comes the cloud," he said.

Annabel didn't even look up. She didn't care about the cloud. She didn't care about the rest of the movie.

Her film career was over.

"Annabel!" her father shouted. "Look!"

She lifted her head.

The movie Annabel was falling to the ground. In slow motion.

"That's the part I messed up. Why did they leave that in?"

The movie Annabel was crying, "Oh, no!" Tears were rolling down her cheeks.

The gray-green cloud swirled around her. There was an eerie whistling sound. Annabel disappeared into the cloud. The cloud whirled back up toward the sky.

The camera pulled back to show all of Central Avenue.

Annabel's red flip-flop was the only thing left on the deserted street.

Everyone in the room burst into applause.

"That was cool!" Oliver said.

"But—" Annabel was too shocked to speak.

Maggie threw her arms around her. "You were incredible!" she said.

"You gave me chills," her father said.

"But it was an accident," Annabel said. "I just fell down. And I never even saw the cloud."

"They put it in later," Oliver said. "Like they told us they would."

"You were *wonderful*," her mother said.

"But I wasn't acting."

Annabel sat back on the couch, still trying to understand what had happened.

Instead of cutting her out of the movie, Steven Roth had focused on her fall and her tears.

She was the only character in the scene who had her own close-up.

"You know what?" Annabel said. "This could be my Big Break after all!"

She jumped off the couch.

"Maybe a famous director is watching the movie right now! And he's saying, 'Who's that poor little girl with one shoe?'"

She grabbed Maggie's hand and pulled her off the couch. "Can't you see it? Then he'll

say, 'That girl is perfect for the part of the pitiful orphan in my next movie!'"

She started whirling Maggie around the room. "I did look pitiful, didn't I?"

"Very pitiful," Maggie panted.

"Oh!" Annabel let go of Maggie's hands. "I

have to write to Winona McCall."

She ran upstairs to her room. She came back with her note paper and a pen.

She flopped onto the floor and pulled out a piece of paper.

"What are you writing to Winona McCall?" Maggie asked.

"A thank-you note," Annabel said. "For helping me to get my Big Break."

She clicked her pen. *"Dear Ms. McCall,"* she wrote.

"But why do you have to write her now?" her mother asked. "The movie is still on."

Annabel looked up from her letter. Her eyes were as bright as the lights on Broadway.

"That's okay," she said. "I already saw the best part."